The MESSY Alphabet Book!

By Erin Guendelsberger

Illustrated by Joe Mathieu

123 SESAME STREET®

sourcebooks jabberwocky

I think it's time
for a new alphabet book,
a MESSY alphabet book.

Turn the page
if you agree.

A is for applesauce dripped down the wall.

B is for birthday cake wrecked by a ball.

C is for cookies all covered in goo.

D is for doughnuts all frosted with glue.

O is for Oscar, the messiest Grouch.

P is for pencils spread out on a couch.

Q is for quilts streaked with permanent ink.

R is for rings around rarely washed sinks.

S is for Slimey, a striped little friend.

T is a tuna fish-marshmallow blend.

U is for unicorns, sparkling and white.

V is for vibrant stars, twinkling at night.

Cover and internal design © 2017 by Sourcebooks, Inc.
Cover illustrations © Sesame Workshop
Text by Erin Guendelsberger
Illustrations by Joe Mathieu

Published by Sourcebooks Jabberwocky, an imprint of Sourcebooks, Inc.
P.O. Box 4410, Naperville, Illinois 60567-4410
(630) 961-3900
Fax: (630) 961-2168
jabberwockykids.com
sourcebooks.com

Source of Production: Leo Paper, Heshan City, Guangdong Province, China.
Date of Production: November 2017
Run Number: 5011268

Printed and bound in China.
LEO 10 9 8 7 6 5 4